library 2000

Illustrated by Vincent Segrelles

Written by Antonio Cunillera

Translated by Jane Inglis

Discoveries and Inventions

FREDERICK WARNE

CONTENTS

INTRODUCTION

Ever since man first appeared on earth, one of his main characteristics has been the urge to find new ideas and a better life. Sometimes his progress has been very rapid, sometimes it has slowed almost to a halt, but for thousands of years he has been observing his surroundings with fascinated interest and analysing the natural phenomena of his world. This kind of study has taken up a great deal of his time. His inventions and discoveries represent the practical results of these centuries of effort. This book sets out to tell you about some of them, and to show how they have helped to change the face of the earth and give man more control over his own destiny.

This book is also about the men whose skill and determination made these scientific inventions and discoveries possible. Some of them must remain anonymous, for we have no written record of mankind's earliest days. In the magnificent illustrations you can see the inventions themselves and also scenes from the daily life of each period. The accompanying text explains each picture in detail.

The astonishing record of what man has achieved by using his intelligence and will is really the record of human history, from prehistoric times right up to the present day.

FIRE

Fire is a discovery rather than an invention. Man had been searching since prehistoric times for a way of making fire easily and quickly, but a really satisfactory answer was found only when tinder-boxes and matches appeared on the scene.

Prehistoric men knew about fire. They must have discovered it by chance, perhaps when lightning caused a fire or when the sun, shining on dry leaves, caused them to ignite. To our ancestors, the discovery of fire was as important as the discovery of electricity or atomic energy has been to us. It was so important that to the primitive mind of early man it seemed holy, a gift from the gods, and became the subject of many myths. In ancient mythology fire worship reappears often.

One of the ways in which prehistoric men made fire was by rubbing two pieces of wood together. It could also be done by rubbing two flint stones together.

Once man had discovered fire, he could warm himself in front of the flames and cook the flesh of animals (previously he had eaten meat raw). Fire brought light into the dark caves. As time went by and men lived in houses, a fire in the hearth helped to create a homely atmosphere.

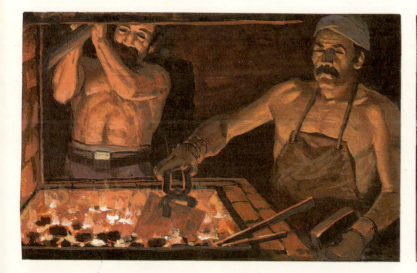

With the aid of fire, men could build furnaces into which they put iron or a variety of other substances, mixed with charcoal. They used bellows to make the fires hotter and so were able to fashion tools for many purposes.

For many centuries man used fire to help him with the tasks of everyday life, although he did not learn to control it completely until the invention of fuel ignition systems, without which modern industry could not function.

Thanks to fire, man was able to manufacture files, saws, axes, hammers, anvils, tongs and deadly weapons. He also learnt how to make glass. So the discovery of fire was of vital importance in the history of humanity. But such a powerful element has its dangers as well as its advantages. It can do us a great deal of good but can also bring about disaster. Think for example of how we heat our buildings: they are comfortable to live in, but if something goes wrong a fire can break out and cause great destruction.

METALS

The period before the discovery and use of metals is called the Neolithic Age. The age of metals began with copper. The first metals to be used were those which occur in the natural state, for example, gold, copper and iron. Then silver and lead were used. Bronze, an alloy of copper and tin, was a great step forward. Thanks to metals, primitive man was able to make a much greater variety of weapons and utensils.

The discovery of copper meant that man could replace his stone tools. Below are shown two pins and a needle made of copper, dating respectively from 2000 BC and 2700 BC. They were found in Cyprus and on Lesbos.

Sumerian period (3000–2000 BC). On the left is a vase and on the right a helmet, both made of gold.

Bull's head in solid copper, found near Ur in Sumer, part of modern Iraq (2800 BC). This is one of the earliest cast objects ever found. Metals were already being used for artistic purposes.

As these examples show, the Sumerian civilization was remarkable for the ornamental pieces it produced, often made of gold and silver. This picture shows a silver chest made by Sumerian craftsmen.

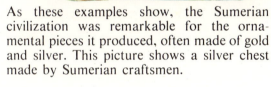

From left to right: bronze statuette from Ur; bronze utensils from the Indus valley; bronze ornament from the Chinese Shang period (1760–1121 BC).

After copper and bronze came iron. Here we see three of the weapons used by men of the Iron Age for fighting.

11

MEGALITHS

Megaliths are enormous stones fixed into the ground and originally erected for religious purposes or to mark some important event in the community. They date from the Neolithic Age and are anything from 5000 to 8000 years old. Many monuments of this kind have been found in Tibet, in India and in the Sahara. They are probably the forerunners of the Egyptian and Mesopotamian obelisks and also of the columns erected by the Romans. Other remarkable monuments of ancient times are the Egyptian pyramids, which prove that those early builders had mastered complicated construction techniques and had all the tools and equipment they needed. The Pharaohs had special roads built so that blocks of stone could be dragged on sledges from the quarry to the building site.

Given the mechanical aids available at that period, the pyramids could only have been built by using an enormous work-force. Egypt possessed a vast army of slaves and besides this public buildings were a state monopoly. Nevertheless it is amazing that such colossal constructions were possible in those distant times with their limited technology. No wonder some people have imagined that extra-terrestrial forces must have been involved in building the pyramids. Today there are still certain primitive tribes that construct megaliths.

The first great monuments in stone date from the Neolithic period. One of the earliest types is the 'menhir', a single vertical stone.

After the menhir, prehistoric man embarked on more complicated constructions in stone. The one above is a 'dolmen' built on the basic principle of a flat horizontal stone supported by vertical pillars.

The sacred monument of Stonehenge, built between 1800 and 1600 BC. Its form indicates that it was used for sun-worship.

The Parthenon (450 BC), is one of the most famous monuments of ancient Greece. The illustration shows a side view of the building. It is an outstanding example of classical Greek architecture.

THE HOUSE

The Neolithic Age brought the first appearance of dwellings which could properly be called houses. They were built in regions where the soil was fertile enough for cultivation. They consisted of huts, either singly or in groups, the floors of which were hollowed out a little below ground level. This partially underground construction had two advantages: it was easier to erect the poles which supported the building, and in winter the temperature inside the hut was higher. Even in Neolithic times houses were sometimes built with several interior rooms, and even with stables and sheds. A special type of town was made up of prehistoric lake dwellings, or palafittes, like the one shown on this page. These were houses built on stilts at the water's edge or on marshy ground, to give protection from wild animals or enemy tribes. Today in the Indian subcontinent there are still tribes living in palafittes. Of all the houses of antiquity (in Greece, Egypt, Mesopotamia or Rome) the Roman house was the best and most comfortable.

In prehistoric times, before man began to build artificial shelters or houses as we understand the word, they lived in caves. Inside these caves it was impossible to make an oven for cooking food. The group generally set up camp at the mouth of the cave or on a rocky ledge nearby. These people may have slept in the caves, but it was on the threshold that they gathered to talk, to fashion their tools, to cut up the spoils of hunting, to prepare their meals, and even to bury their dead.

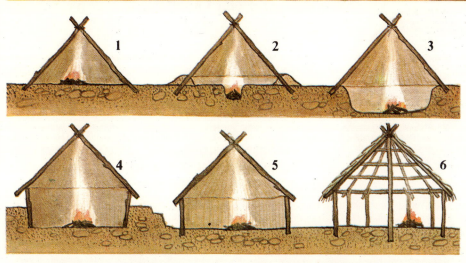

Primitive hut with a fire made on the centre of the floor (1); hut with hollowed out hearth in the centre and with perimeter walls reinforced (2 and 3); hut with walls and foundations (4 and 5); fully evolved hut (6).

After huts man developed buildings made of baked bricks. Shown here is part of a city in the Indus valley of 2000 BC.

Nowadays many people live in blocks of flats. Modern blocks are often built of reinforced concrete. This consists of large sections of concrete with steel rods embedded in it to give added strength.

THE ALPHABET

Ever since the dawn of language and thought man must have felt the need to record his ideas and emotions in some permanent form, and he has continued to look for ways of doing this right up to the present day with its gramophone records and magnetic tape. An old Latin saying proves the point: 'The spoken word is forgotten but the written word remains.'

The first alphabets were developed among the populations devoted to agriculture and stock-raising in China, India, Mesopotamia, Egypt and Central America. In Chinese, writing does not approach the name of a thing by breaking its sound down into letters and syllables but sets out to express the thing itself. Written words are direct representations of things or ideas (ideographs) or of particular spoken words (logographs). A different ideograph evolved for each object. So the Chinese language is based on an enormous number of different characters rather than on the letters of an alphabet.

The illustration below shows an Egyptian scribe, whose job was to record the dates and events of each Pharaoh's reign. He wrote in hieroglyphics on papyrus leaves.

Above is an example of Egyptian hieroglyphic writing. It was used only by the priests and the royal court. Below: the simpler demotic writing used by the people.

Did you know . . .

. . . that the famous Rosetta stone, discovered by Napoleon's soldiers and deciphered by the scholar Champollion, provided the clue to the secret of Egyptian hieroglyphic writing?

. . . that the modern Western alphabet is based, with some modifications, on that of the Phoenicians, a seafaring and mercantile people?

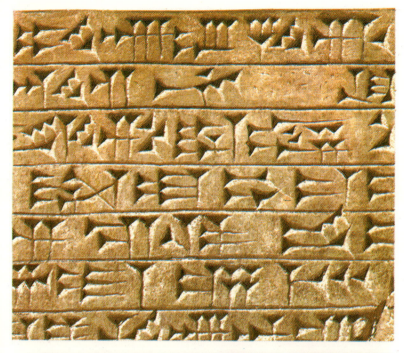

Sumerian writing dates back to 4000 BC and is the most ancient writing known today. It is characterized by its wedge-shaped appearance and is called 'cuneiform' from the Latin word *cuneus*, meaning 'a wedge'. This alphabet enabled men to collect the first libraries. On the left is some Assyrian writing from the eighth century BC. As the illustration shows, the Assyro-Babylonians adopted cuneiform characters from the conquered Sumerians, and its use spread among other contemporary peoples.

ALPHABETS		
Phoenician	Greek	Latin
	A	A
	B	B
	Δ	D
	E	E
	H	H
	K	K
	Λ	L
	M	M
	N	N
	O	O
	P	R
	Σ	S
	T	T

This illustration shows a bas-relief of a warrior with his spear. The inscription is in Greek. The Greek alphabet can be seen as the link between the ancient alphabets of the Mediterranean world and the alphabet of today. It is worth noting that the Greek alphabet already had 24 signs.

This table compares three alphabets. Notice the similarity between many of the Greek and Latin letters (in capitals).

On the left is a Bivort shorthand machine (French, 1902). It enabled writing to keep up with the speed of speech. The fountain-pen was invented by Bion in 1854, and the typewriter was invented by the Austrian Mitterhofer in 1882.

MONEY

If people have too much of one thing and not enough of another, they can use their surplus goods in exchange for the products that they need. This system is called barter, and men have been using it since the earliest times. Later, metals and precious jewels came to be used to replace this simple exchange. The metals were used in the form of ingots (especially gold and silver because of their special properties: they are imperishable, consistent in quality, easy to break up and have a high value for a small weight). In antiquity the Phoenicians were the most outstanding commercial race, buying and selling an amazing variety of products. The Hindu sacred books or Vedas and the Book of Genesis in the Bible mention this type of primitive money (metal ingots). The first coins were minted in Lydia in the seventh century BC and were called 'electrons'. As money improved the coins took the form of small discs which became progressively rounder and flatter. Some ancient coins include the Athenian drachma (a silver coin), the Macedonian talent, the Roman denarius and sestertius, the besant of the Middle Ages, the maravedi, doubloon and crown of medieval Christian Spain. In the nineteenth century the circulation of paper money became general.

Did you know . . .

. . . that the word 'money' comes from the Latin *Moneta*, the surname of the goddess Juno in whose temple coins were made?

The ox was once the basic unit of barter. It was equivalent to a piece of copper shaped like an ox hide and weighing up to 30kg.

In commerce, barter was practised by exchanging raw materials for manufactured goods, greatly to the advantage of the manufacturer.

Raw materials such as minerals and grains were exchanged for manufactured goods such as pottery, harpoons, fish-hooks, glassware and a great variety of other products.

A series of ancient coins. Notice how the primitive crudeness gradually disappears and how the coins become rounder. From left to right: almond-shaped gold ingot weighing 8.5g; gilt coin of Augustus Caesar, Emperor of Rome; silver coin of Ramon Borrell II; 8-crown coin of Philip V of Spain, minted in Mexico; peseta of 1869.

Swedish bank note of 1717. Once these notes were issued it became possible to pay debts without large amounts of ready money.

Five-peso note, issued in Cuba in 1896. Many years had passed since the first primitive paper money. This one already looks quite like a present-day bank note.

PAPER

Once the alphabet had been invented, man could write; but what was he to write on? He needed to find something on which information could be preserved indefinitely, something stable and durable, something easy to handle which was at the same time fairly tough but not too difficult to tear, and as light as possible so that it could be easily transported. Smooth rock surfaces were the first 'paper' used by mankind. Remember that prehistoric men drew and painted on the stone walls of their caves. Inscriptions on stone were very short, exhausting for their author and had the enormous disadvantage of being impossible to move. The same difficulty applies to tree trunks, which are used by some primitive peoples to this day. Before the arrival of paper as we know it a whole series of writing surfaces were invented using materials such as clay tablets, papyrus, waxed tablets and parchment.

Today paper is one of the mainsprings of our civilization. It is said that the standard of living of a country can be measured by the amount of paper it consumes. Without paper there would be no books, no magazines, no newspapers, no notebooks . . . and so on. Thanks to paper, man has at his disposal one of the most convenient methods of communication. There can be no doubt that the invention of paper was one of the most important events in the history of humanity.

The Babylonians invented tablets made of clay or mud on which they wrote with a stylus. The tablets were then baked.

The ancient Egyptians used papyrus, a substance derived from the plant of the same name, which has a triangular stem enveloped in a membrane which may be as much as 1m in length.

The Greeks and Romans had a different method of writing. They took notes on waxed tablets by means of a pointed instrument which pierced the layer cf wax.

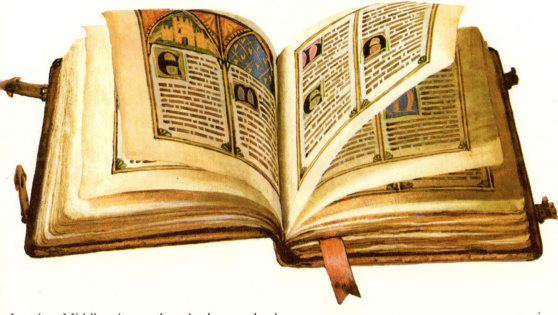

About 300 BC a war broke out between the kingdoms of Pergamum and Egypt. Eumenes, monarch of Pergamum, ordered his subjects to find a material which could replace Egyptian papyrus. The learned men of the kingdom discovered a substance made from sheep skin. The wool was removed and the hide was scraped, beaten and stretched. It became known as 'parchment', derived from the name of the country.

In the Middle Ages the Arabs made known throughout Muslim Spain a material which was to replace all its predecessors. This was paper, whose manufacture they imported from the far distant and mysterious realm of China.

The first paper appeared in China about 200 BC. Its name is derived from papyrus. Silk was transformed into paper by a process of pasting, but because silk was expensive, wool and cotton came to be used instead. This invention was attributed to Ts'ai Lun.

On the right is shown the manufacturing process used by the Chinese. They steeped mulberry or bamboo bark in water, then kneaded it to produce a paste from which they obtained smooth thin sheets of paper.

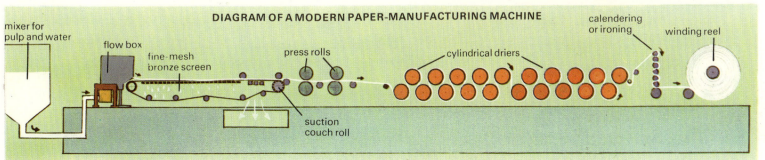

DIAGRAM OF A MODERN PAPER-MANUFACTURING MACHINE

mixer for pulp and water

flow box

fine-mesh bronze screen

press rolls

suction couch roll

cylindrical driers

calendering or ironing

winding reel

THE COMPASS

In the second century BC the compass was already known in China, but it was not used for navigation. The Arabs inherited it not from the Chinese but from the West. Literary evidence proves that the compass was known and used at the end of the twelfth century. Its use by navigators was limited until the day when the magnetic needle more or less freely suspended was united with a 'wind rose' or card on which the directions were marked. This great improvement is attributed to the Italian Flavio Gioia of Amalfi (about 1300). Thanks to the compass, ships could now take their bearings and avoid shipwreck.

The compass is an instrument for finding direction based on the property of a magnetic needle of settling on a north–south line. The needle swings on a central pivot above a disc marked with the cardinal points. A ship's compass hung on gimbals will maintain its horizontal position in spite of the movement of the ship. The compass card, showing the desired direction of travel, completes the instrument.

The quadrant is a primitive direction-finding instrument. Its invention is attributed to the famous Greek astronomer Anaximander in the sixth century BC.

Another instrument used for navigational purposes long ago was the cross-staff. It measured the angle of the stars and consisted of a graded staff along which a sliding cross-piece could be moved.

Astrolabe for observing the position of the stars and measuring their height above the horizon.

The compass shows the position of magnetic north, which forms an angle of magnetic declination with true north, while the direction of travel is given by the axis of the ship. Petrus Peregrinus de Maricourt produced the first study of the compass in his *Epistola de Magnete* (Chapter on Magnetism) of 1269. After this the compass was improved by stages until it reached the perfection of the magnetic steering compass which gives the best possible indication of a ship's course. Many earlier versions led up to this achievement.

A modern sextant used to judge a ship's position at sea. It has a scale of 60°, one sixth of the earth's circumference, and works by measuring the angle of the stars.

Marine chronometer, a timepiece used on board ship. The exact measurement of time is very important for finding one's position at sea. It is rather bulky and is kept in a special box.

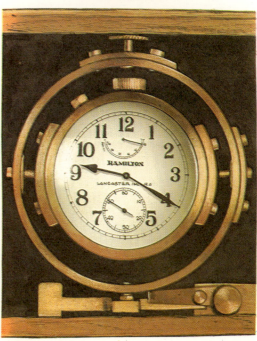

THE POST

The need for a postal service so that commands and proclamations could be broadcast rapidly was recognized very early in the history of mankind. Such a service existed in the empires of Persia and Assyria a thousand years before Christ, but it was exclusively for the use of the rulers. The Greeks used relays of professional runners to carry really important news. In Roman times, thanks to the magnificent communication system, the post became very important. There was also a private postal service operated by slaves. The ancient and mysterious empire of China always had an important postal system, and so did the vast empire of the Incas in Peru. During the Middle Ages the postal system remained undeveloped, and it was not until the fourteenth century that a public service for the use of ordinary citizens became available.

The postal deliveries of the fifteenth century were made on horseback, and were replaced in the seventeenth century by vehicles. The service was improved in the nineteenth century and increased in scope. All this cost money, so postal charges had been introduced by the end of the sixteenth century.

Did you know . . .

. . . that a postal service was set up in the fifteenth century by the Tassis or Taxis family, of Italian origin?

Roman chariot. Next to the driver sat a postal official who was in charge of the mail carried.

The stamp represents the postal tax which brings in the revenue necessary to run a postal service. This is the famous 'Penny black', the first postage stamp ever issued (1840).

The postage stamp was such a success in England that it was copied widely. Here for example is the first Spanish stamp, which was issued in 1850.

Rowland Hill's idea was a universal success. The postal services became more and more important as time went on, and there were numerous issues of stamps.

The Englishman, Rowland Hill, creator of the modern postal system. The first postage stamps were issued in Great Britain as a result of his pioneering work.

In the far West of the United States the fame of the Pony Express, which collected and delivered the mail, became legendary.

An English mail coach of 1790. Deliveries were often delayed and even lost because of bad roads.

In its long history the postal service gradually evolved through the various stages of the chariot, the messenger, the horse and the mail coach. Today every modern means of transport is used for postal deliveries. Aeroplanes, ships, trains and motor vehicles enable the most distant parts of the world to be reached rapidly.

On the right is shown a post box from which letters are taken to an office to be sorted and distributed. In 1874 the Universal Postal Union was set up in Berne and since then a letter, prepaid by means of a stamp, can reach any corner of the globe.

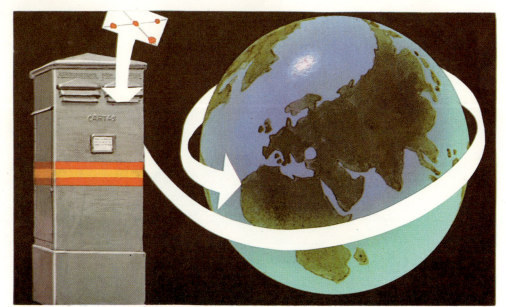

THE STEAM ENGINE

Man's first major source of energy was a product of fire and water. Hero of Alexandria invented the aeolipile or wind-valve, and entertained his fellow citizens with its turning sphere. The machine consisted of a hollow sphere pivoted so that it could revolve on its axis. A curved spout protruded at each end of a line perpendicular to the axis. Water in the cauldron below was heated to supply steam to the sphere, which began to revolve as the steam emerged from spouts. This little invention can be considered the forerunner of the steam engine. Later, from the seventeenth century, scientists, such as Torricelli, Pascal, Guericke, Huygens, Papin, Savery, Newcomen and Watt, started on the series of investigations which led up to the invention of an efficient steam engine. The successful invention of the steam engine was the end product of much hard work and experimentation.

The steam engine and all its applications helped to change the world in the same way as the discoveries of fire, electricity and atomic energy have done. The steam is produced in a boiler and introduced into a closed cylinder containing a piston which is subjected to the pressure of the steam, sometimes distributed by a valve, so that it moves backwards and forwards. This motion is transferred via a connecting rod to the crankshaft, which is caused to rotate.

Denis Papin, a Frenchman, devised the primitive form of boiler shown on the left. It had strong walls and a safety valve. Papin's was the earliest cylinder-and-piston steam engine (below).

Cross-section of Newcomen's steam engine seen at the moment when the cold water is introduced into the cylinder. This machine was constructed in 1712 by the Englishmen Thomas Newcomen and John Cawley. It was used to pump water out of mines. It had to be manned by a workman to open two valves, one controlling the arrival of the steam in the cylinder and the other controlling the arrival of the water to condense the steam. A young lad called Humphrey Potter was given this job. He saw what nobody else had realized — that the machine was capable of operating the two valves by itself. It was simply a matter of winding one end of a rope round the valves and fastening the other at exactly the right point on the beam. Having put this plan into effect he was free to go off and play with his friends.

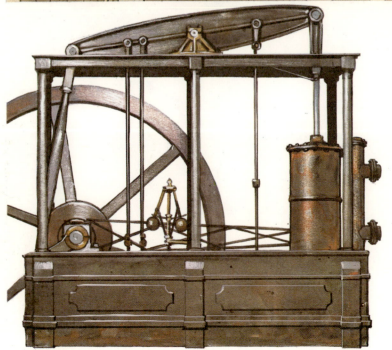

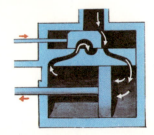 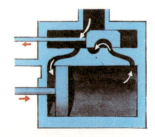

A diagram of James Watt's steam engine in action is shown above. Once perfected by its inventor, this engine supplied the power for the industry of the nineteenth century. This was the dawn of the age of steam. Left is an example of a low-pressure engine already equipped with a condenser.

VACCINES

Vaccination was first carried out by the English doctor and naturalist Edward Jenner (1749–1823), born at Berkeley in Gloucestershire. In the picture he is shown with the symbol of death, a cow and a syringe. Jenner had heard of a popular belief in Gloucestershire that a person who had accidentally contracted pustules by milking a cow infected with cowpox (known in Latin as *vaccinia*, hence the name for the treatment) would be immune from smallpox. So, in 1796, he began to use the matter from cowpox pustules. At first the discovery met with a barrage of prejudiced opposition, but during the nineteenth century the practice of vaccination spread all over Europe. Vaccines are produced by weakening viruses by various different means, including heat, light and ultra-violet rays. Vaccines are now available to prevent not only smallpox but many other diseases such as tetanus, diphtheria, typhoid, polio and whooping-cough.

Did you know . . .

. . . that the greatest doctor of the ancient world was the Greek Hippocrates, and that doctors today still take the 'Hippocratic oath'?

. . . that during the Middle Ages knowledge of medicine was preserved in the Benedictine monasteries?

. . . that following a campaign by the World Health Organization smallpox has been completely eliminated from the world?

28

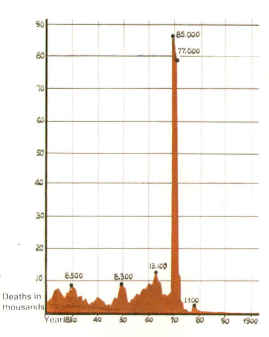

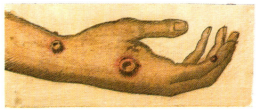

Hand of the milkmaid Sarah Nelmes showing cowpox pustules.

Chart showing smallpox deaths in England. Notice the peak figures due to the epidemic of 1871.

Jenner inoculated a child's arm with matter from cowpox pustules. The patient developed pustules similar to those of infected cattle, and acquired immunity from smallpox.

Louis Pasteur, one of the founding fathers of bacteriology. Working in his laboratory on animals infected with rabies, he obtained an attenuated (weakened) virus to combat the disease.

The electronic microscope has been invaluable in the field of bacteriology research. Scientists can use it to observe organisms of ultramicroscopic size. Here we see a modern instrument 4m high weighing 22 tonnes. It is capable of magnifying 100,000 times. This is an example of science and technology working hand in hand to advance medical research.

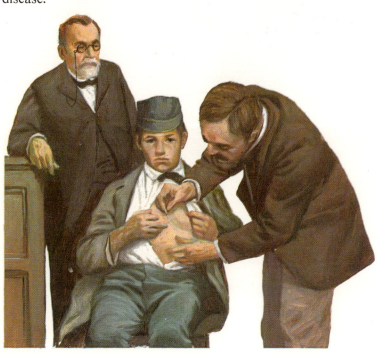

Pasteur devoted his whole life to research and discovered not only bacteria, which cause many illnesses, but also the means of fighting them. He developed the process — known as pasteurization — of destroying harmful germs by heat. The illustration shows his successful and famous treatment in 1885 of young Joseph Meister, who was bitten by a mad dog. His life was saved by Pasteur's vaccine.

THE COLT REVOLVER

Barrel of revolver, bullet, cartridge and percussion cap.

The most important name in the history of the revolver is that of Samuel Colt. Even as a boy he was fascinated by weapons and explosives, and at the age of ten he tried to build a four-barrelled gun whose barrels would revolve. The attempt failed, but it taught him some useful lessons. His revolvers were patented in England and France in 1835 and a year later in the United States. A company was formed to produce them, but the factory at Paterson, New Jersey, had to close down before long. Then, in 1847, Colt's luck changed when the United States Army adopted the Colt revolver, which was so powerful that it could bring down a man or an animal with one shot.

Did you know . . .

. . . that Colt's father did not want his son to spend his life making weapons, and tried to prevent it by sending him to sea as a cabin boy on a ship bound for the Indies?

. . . that the idea for his revolver came to Colt while he was looking at the helm of a boat? Whatever the angle of the tiller there was always a hand-grip within reach, and Colt thought that the same rotary principle could perhaps be applied to a firearm.

Colt percussion revolver, 1849

Colt revolver with metal cartridge, model P (1873)

Collier revolver, 1819

Nineteenth-century pistol with revolving cylinders

The American engineer Samuel Colt was born in Hartford in 1814 and died in 1862.

Colt raised the money for the work on his invention by carrying out public demonstrations of explosions caused by nitrous oxide.

In 1830, before building his weapon, Colt made a model of it in wood. The picture shows the three basic components of his weapon.

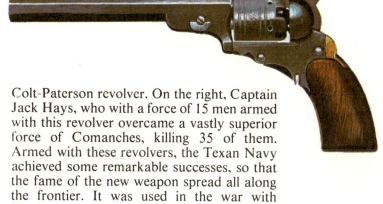
Colt-Paterson revolver. On the right, Captain Jack Hays, who with a force of 15 men armed with this revolver overcame a vastly superior force of Comanches, killing 35 of them. Armed with these revolvers, the Texan Navy achieved some remarkable successes, so that the fame of the new weapon spread all along the frontier. It was used in the war with Mexico.

Buntline-Colt, 1876, with its detachable butt and long barrel. Sheriff Wyatt Earp used this gun; it was a present from Nell Buntline, biographer of the famous adventurer Buffalo Bill.

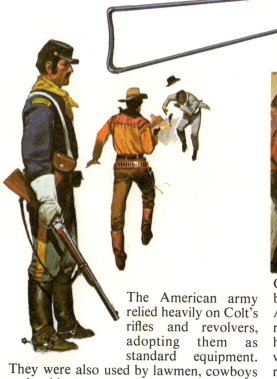
The American army relied heavily on Colt's rifles and revolvers, adopting them as standard equipment. They were also used by lawmen, cowboys and gold prospectors.

Colt set up a factory for producing his weapons in London, but it failed because of competition from the English Adams revolver, which was less accurate and shorter in range, but quicker-firing since it was automatic. During the heavy fighting of the Crimean War when enemy positions were being stormed, the superior speed of the Adams revolver was clearly proved, and the American engineer returned home disappointed.

General Patton bought two model P Colts in 1916 and fought with them during two world wars. Although this model went out of production it continued to be highly prized.

31

THE TELEGRAPH

For many thousands of years men had no means of speaking to each other across great distances, although there had been various methods of communication based on sight or sound. These included the tom-tom, the trumpet, bells, banners, beacons, smoke signals, torches and mirrors to reflect the sun's rays. But all these methods were of limited range.

Samuel Morse was the inventor of the telegraph. He built his first apparatus in 1835. The illustration below shows the final version of the Morse receiver, which he perfected in 1852. The basic components of this apparatus were a battery from which the current ran along the telegraph wire forming a circuit, a transmitter, and a receiver which marked on a moving paper strip the dots and dashes of the Morse alphabet. This alphabet, known as the Morse code, is still in use today. Morse and his team of two technicians had struggled to devise an alphabet in which letters were replaced by dots and dashes. They were eventually successful, and made their first trials over 16km.

Did you know . . .

. . . that Samuel Morse would never have invented the telegraph if the American government had accepted his paintings? Denied access to an artistic career, he turned instead to his favourite hobby and devoted himself to experimental work in physics and electricity.

. . . that the first telegraph message was transmitted by Morse from Washington to Baltimore in 1844 and read 'What hath God wrought?'?

. . . that Morse used his easel as the armature of the first telegraph apparatus he built?

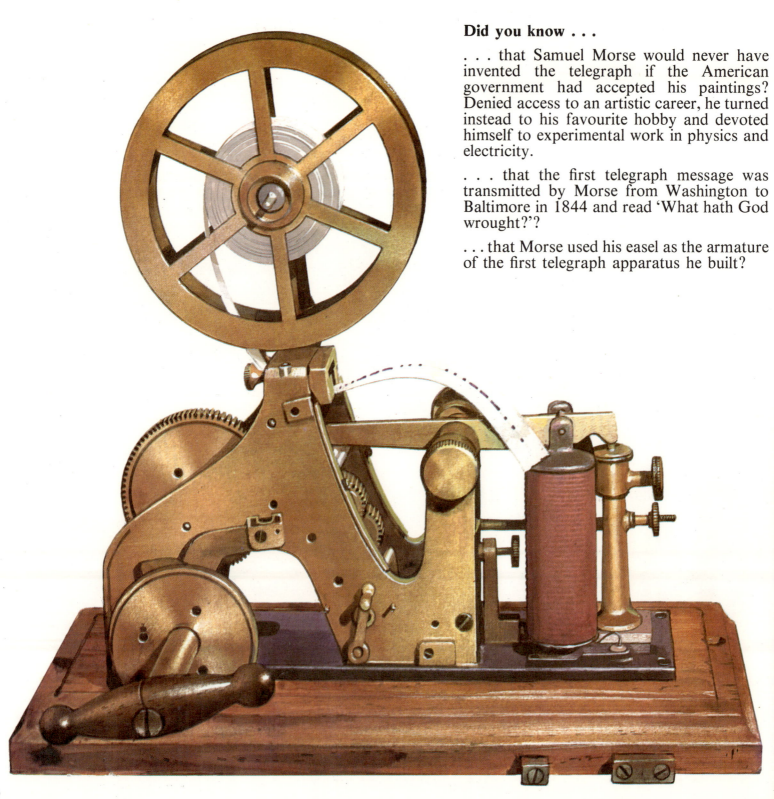

Telegraph apparatus of classical times invented by Aeneas Tacticus. It consisted of two identical vessels filled with water, one placed at the transmitting end and one at the receiving end. Signs corresponding to various messages were engraved on a board. Visual signals were exchanged to indicate the exact moment at which the two taps should be turned on and off. The news transmitted by this curious apparatus was given by the sign touching water level at the moment when the taps were turned off.

Chappe's telegraph, 1791. The upper part of the apparatus was made up of a movable arm and two levers to adjust its position. Each position indicated a letter.

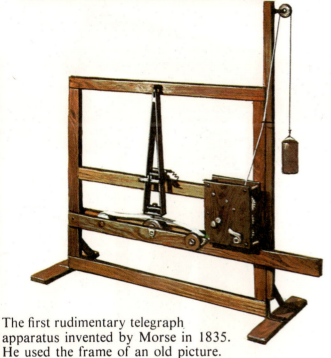

The first rudimentary telegraph apparatus invented by Morse in 1835. He used the frame of an old picture.

The famous English transatlantic ship *Great Eastern* was specially chartered to lay the first submarine telegraph cable between Europe and America. This first attempt was a failure because the connection was unsatisfactory, but later the two continents were successfully linked by submarine cable.

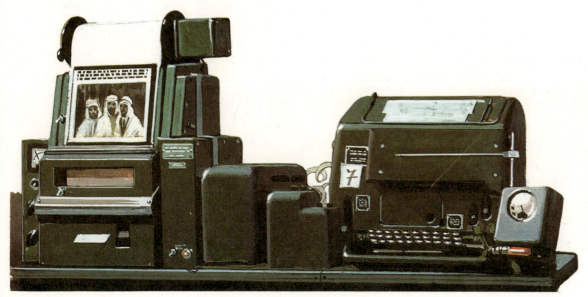

Once intercontinental telegraph links had been established, scientists began to wonder whether it might be possible for the dots and dashes of the Morse code to be replaced by the human voice itself. And so it was, with the invention of the telephone. But this was not the end of the story of the telegraph. The illustration shows two later developments based on the principle of telegraphy. On the right is a teleprinter, a machine which can transmit typewritten messages in the space of seconds, and on the left is a phototelegraph, an instrument which transmits photographs.

PETROLEUM

We have no idea how long ago men first found petroleum or mineral oil. What may be the earliest reference to its use occurs in a Chinese chronicle of the third century BC. A mine shaft dug for the extraction of rock salt was illuminated by a primitive lighting system, but the deposit became exhausted and its existence was forgotten. The Byzantines used an oily liquid with an unpleasant smell 'which burnt in the water' against the Turkish fleet when it attacked Constantinople. Bundles of tow were soaked in this oil and then used most successfully as missiles against the enemy. The oil came from Baku in Armenia, where it had been discovered by the engineer Callinico. The picture below shows oil-extracting machinery and a derrick.

Did you know . . .

. . . that when the apothecary Samuel Kier saw Indians using oil as a medicine, he started selling bottles of a mysterious liquid which he claimed would cure bronchitis?

. . . that in 1840 the Russian governor of Baku sent some oil samples to the Academy of Science in St Petersburg? The Academy's verdict was that the product might be useful for greasing cart wheels!

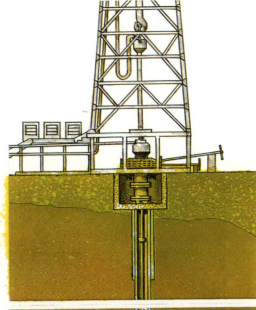

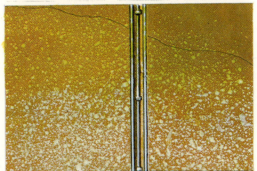

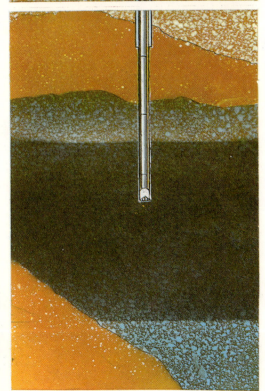

Petroleum is a vital source of energy all over the world. It is carried across country by means of oil pipelines.

The flow of crude oil is made possible by using pipes with spiral grooves. Water is added to the oil and forms an outer layer just inside the pipe, preventing loss of pressure due to friction.

Petroleum is carried across the oceans by huge tankers; but oil spillage has become a major problem.

Crude oil has to be refined. On the right is a refinery for the distillation of crude petroleum.

The picture shows a rotary drilling rig which explores for oil and digs wells. Two of the world's largest oil companies are Standard Oil (Esso), founded by John D. Rockefeller (USA), and the Anglo-Dutch company Royal Dutch Shell, largely the creation of Henri Deterding.

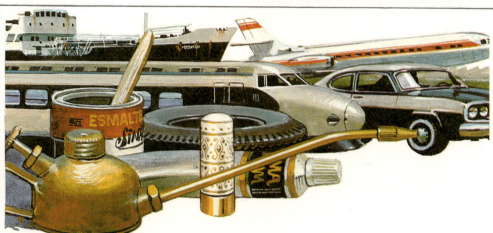

Many products are derived from petroleum. They include motor fuels such as naphtha, petrol and benzine; detergents, solvents, insecticides, synthetic fibres, cosmetics, medicines, plastics, fertilizers, paints, lubricants, asphalt, synthetic rubber, and many others.

THE PROPELLER

The basic idea of the propeller is the same as that of the turbine (see p. 42). The difference arises from the fact that instead of converting a flow of fluid into energy, it acts as a means of propulsion. It consists of two or more blades with spiral surfaces arranged radially round an axis. A controversy arose in the propeller's early days as to whether it was superior to paddles as a means of propulsion. The question was answered in 1845 when a propeller constructed by an Englishman called Smith was fitted for the first time on to a British ship, the HMS *Rattler* (888 tonnes), and this ship was attached stern to stern to the *Alecto* (800 tonnes) which was driven by paddles. The two ships were equal in power, with 200hp engines, and floated at the same waterline. It was clear from the start that the propeller-driven ship had the best of it, and the *Rattler* was easily able to tow its rival. The success of the propeller was guaranteed from then on.

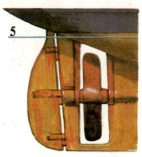

Five successive stages in the evolution of the propeller.
1 Early propeller by Shorter, 1800. **2** Smith's screw-propeller, 1836. It proved fragile and was therefore shortened — **3**. **4** Steven's double contrarotating propeller. **5** Ericson's propeller of 1839, almost identical to a modern propeller.

A giant propeller as fitted on large ships compared with the size of a human figure. In 1858 the *Great Eastern* was launched. It was the largest ship ever built at that time and its propeller was 7.31m in diameter.

The first attempt to use the propeller to drive lighter-than-air craft was probably made by Giffard, who used a steam engine. The propeller became more and more popular and played an important part in the development of aviation.

An up-to-date model of a ship's propeller developed by the United States Navy. It is called a 'super-cavitating' propeller and makes use of cavitation (the formation of a space filled with water vapour round the turning blades of the propeller) to gain increased speed. In earlier models speed had been cut down by the pocket of bubbles caused by the propeller's eddy.

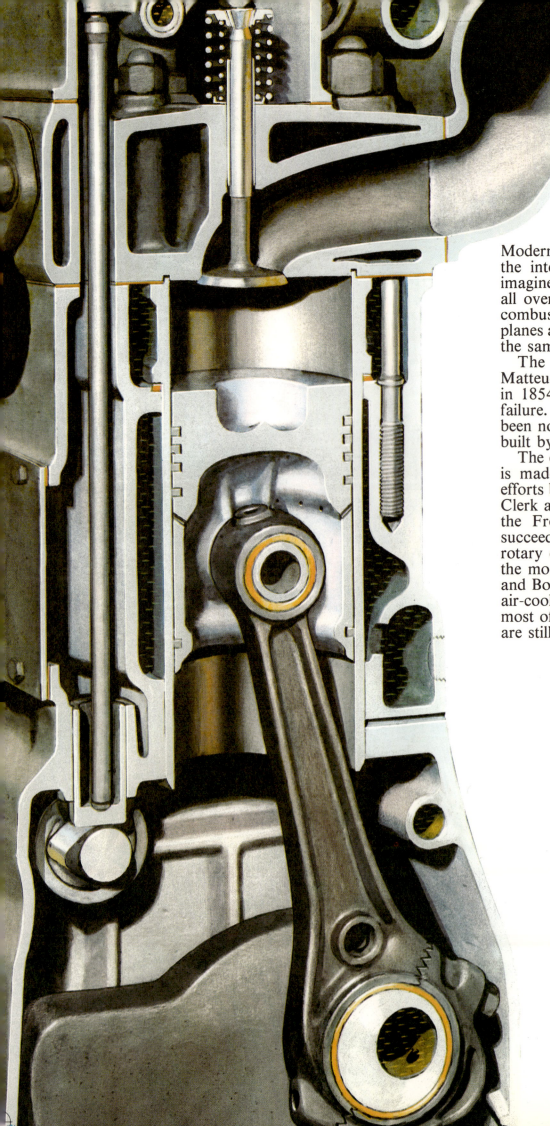

THE INTERNAL COMBUSTION ENGINE

Modern civilization is entirely dependent on the internal combustion engine. Just try to imagine life without the thousands of vehicles all over the world which run on the internal combustion engine, not to mention the ships, planes and other machines which are driven by the same type of engine.

The Italian physicists Barsanti and Matteucci invented the first combustion engine in 1854, but for practical purposes it was a failure. An earlier attempt by Huygens had been no more successful and the later model built by Lenoir was not very efficient.

The early history of the combustion engine is made up of a series of experiments and efforts by such men as Beau de Rochas, Otto, Clerk and Diesel. Also worthy of mention are the Frenchman Félix Millet who in 1893 succeeded in fitting a small motorcycle with a rotary engine with a fixed crankshaft, one of the most difficult engines to build, and Dion and Bouton who in 1894 built a one-cylinder air-cooled engine of a type which was fitted on most of the early motor cars. Similar engines are still in use today to drive motorcycles.

Did you know . . .

. . . that at the end of the eighteenth century engineers like James Watt already knew how to build an internal combustion engine, but were unable to do so because they had no fuel capable of igniting in a fraction of a second inside a closed space?

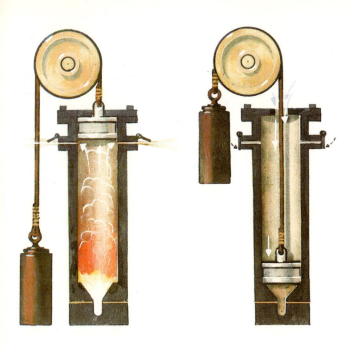

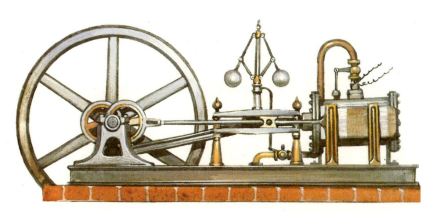

In 1673 the Dutch physicist Christiaan Huygens designed the machine on the left which worked by using air and gunpowder. He thought that he might be able to use it to propel vehicles. It was never actually built. Below is shown Etienne Lenoir's internal combustion engine, which was not unlike the steam engines of the period. It ran on gas with electric ignition but was never a very efficient machine.

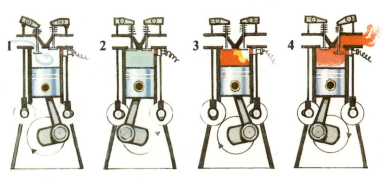

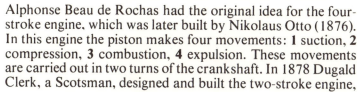

Alphonse Beau de Rochas had the original idea for the four-stroke engine, which was later built by Nikolaus Otto (1876). In this engine the piston makes four movements: 1 suction, 2 compression, 3 combustion, 4 expulsion. These movements are carried out in two turns of the crankshaft. In 1878 Dugald Clerk, a Scotsman, designed and built the two-stroke engine,

which functions in a simpler way. In this engine the cycle is completed in one turn of the crankshaft. It is mainly used for motorbikes. On the right is Felix Wankel's rotary engine. The pistons are replaced by a triangular rotor which carries out all four strokes in one revolution. Wankel's rotary piston engine is used in cars and aeroplanes.

On the left: Rudolf Diesel, who invented a new type of internal combustion engine in 1892; and one of the first diesel engines, built in Switzerland in 1903. This engine drove a pump and worked for ten hours a day right up to 1951.

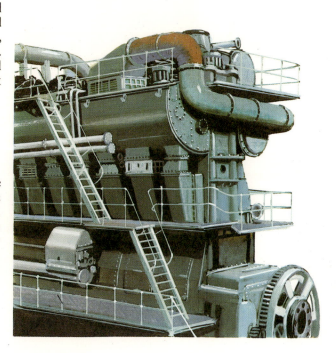

On the right: a ship's engine room. The diesel engine is particularly suitable for ships. The picture shows a 16,800hp diesel engine (135 strokes per minute). This engine is better in some ways than the steam turbine, although it is less powerful. Engines based on Diesel's ignition principle were fitted on many early motor cars.

ELECTROMAGNETIC MACHINES

Electricity has been known to man since ancient times. Thales of Miletus wrote about it in detail in the sixth century BC. Man must always have been fascinated by this mysterious force which was known long ago as 'energy of the gods'. In 1600 William Gilbert realized that electricity was in fact an independent natural force, and gave it its name. From that day to this scientists have continued to study and harness electricity. Otto von Guericke invented the electrostatic machine, and in 1727 Gray discovered that electricity could be carried from one place to another. Von Kleist invented the Leyden jar, which made it possible to store this invisible source of power. Knowledge of electromagnetism was advanced by the experiments and theories of many other scientists, among them Galvani, Volta, Coulomb, Faraday, Ohm and Oersted. Werner von Siemens was another outstanding figure. He was in prison for acting as second in a duel, and in the solitude of his cell he discovered a method of gilding and silvering metals by electroplating and gave his process the name 'galvanizing bath'. In 1867 he completed the invention to which he owes his fame: the dynamo or electromagnetic generator. Any account of the dynamo should also mention the names of Pacinotti and Gramme. Below is shown the dynamo-electric machine invented by Gramme in 1870. Such machines are enormously important in the modern world.

The picture on the left shows the great English physicist Michael Faraday, who discovered electromagnetic induction. By introducing a magnet into a solenoid (a coil of wire) he found a revolutionary method of generating electricity.

We owe the invention of the dynamo, a machine which can generate electricity and function as a motor, to the Italian Pacinotti. The picture on the right shows the Belgian Z. T. Gramme who followed up the work of Pacinotti and built another type of dynamo.

At the Vienna Exhibition of 1873 an engineer named Fontaine was in charge of Gramme's stand. There was one dynamo to provide a current and behind it another generator in reserve in case of a breakdown. But a workman connected the two machines together by mistake. Fontaine had a sudden brainwave and asked for the cables to be lengthened as much as possible. He set up the reserve generator at the far end of the cable. As soon as the other end was connected to the first generator, the second came to life, 250m distant. This discovery led to electricity being carried over long distances, and Gramme's generator became the long-awaited electric motor.

On the left is a modern electricity generator powered by a hydraulic turbine. Below are shown several other types of electric motor used today.

THE TURBINE

In general terms, a turbine is a machine for converting the kinetic energy of a paddle wheel or the pressure of a fluid or gas into mechanical energy in the form of rotary movement. The driving force may be steam, wind or gas. After the invention of the steam engine, the appearance of the steam turbine represented one more step up the ladder in man's exploitation of energy. This turbine was produced in the second half of the nineteenth century when the English inventor Charles Parsons succeeded in applying to industry the principle of designs made in the second century BC by the Greek Hero of Alexandria. It was called the reaction turbine because the expansion of the steam took place among moving blades. In contrast, the Swedish inventor De Laval's turbine had both fixed and moving parts. The illustration below shows the steam turbine rotor designed by Parsons.

Did you know . . .

. . . that the first locomotive driven by a gas turbine was built in 1941 by Brown Bovery for the Swiss Federal Railways?

. . . that in 1956 the *John Sergeant* (16,000 tonnes) became the first ship propelled by gas turbines?

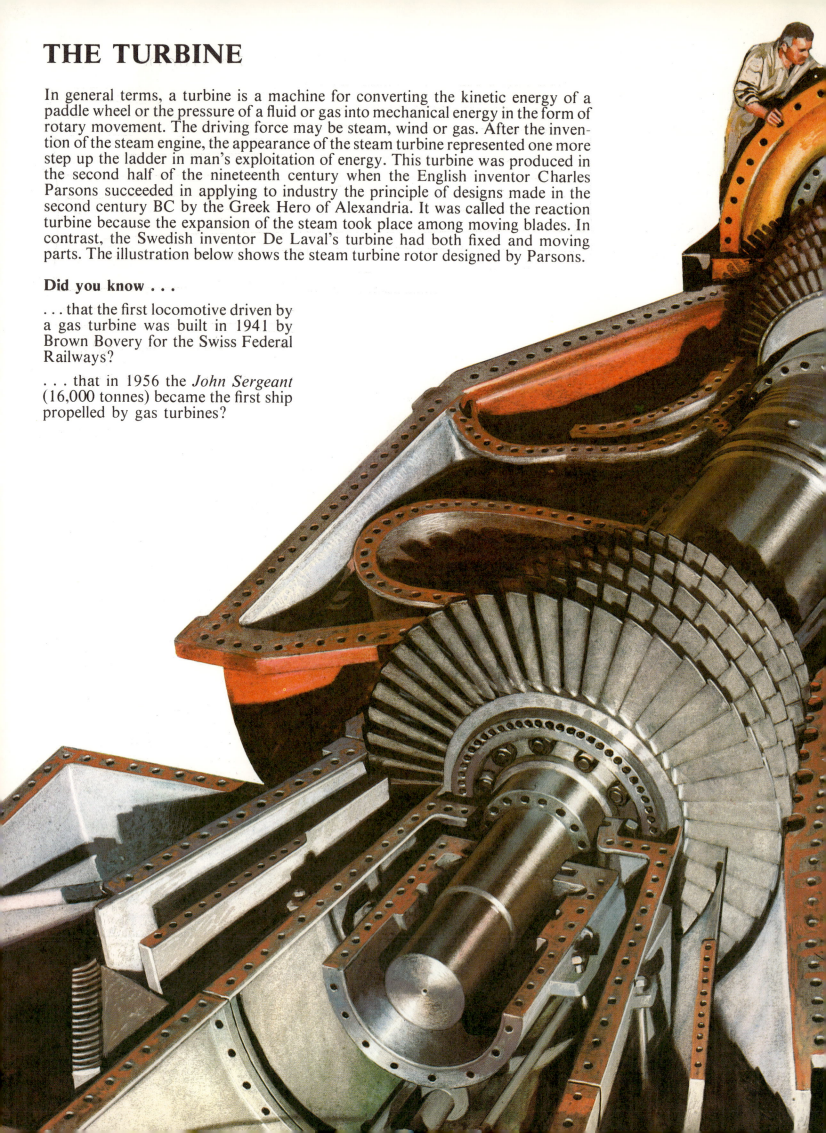

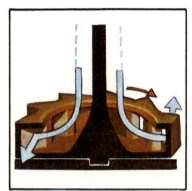

The ancestor of our modern turbine is the hydraulic wheel of ancient times. The oldest hydraulic engine was the 'undershot wheel'.

Between classical times and the Middle Ages the 'overshot wheel' was developed, to use the weight of the water.

The first true example of a reaction turbine was Segner's wheel (1750). The water flows into a cylinder and flows out through tangential openings.

Fourneyron's turbine is equipped with a distributor to direct the water and ensure that it acts on the blades of the wheel as efficiently as possible.

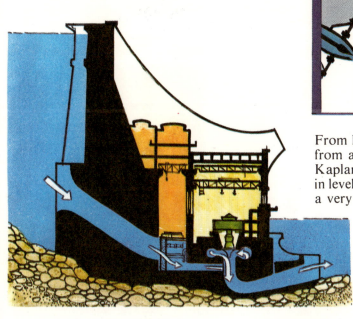

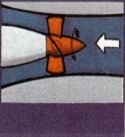

From left to right: Pelton turbine for use where a small volume of water falls from a great height; Francis turbine for falls of medium height and volume; Kaplan turbine with propeller for large volumes of water without much change in level (tide-driven generating stations, and rivers with a large flow of water but a very gradual loss of level).

The modern Francis turbine is named after James Francis and based on the first radial reaction turbine with an external distributor, which he invented in 1840. The illustration shows a dam with a Francis turbine used to generate electricity.

The first steam turbines to be manufactured on an industrial scale were those of the Swedish engineer De Laval.

In 1897 the world was amazed when the little British ship *Turbinia* achieved a speed of 34.5 knots. It was fitted with Parsons steam turbines which supplied 2000hp divided among nine propellers.

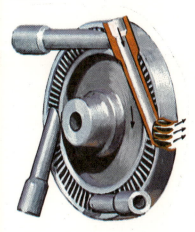

THE HELICOPTER

Apart from Leonardo da Vinci's contribution to the story of aviation, there were many other precursors of the modern helicopter. Colonel Renard made a close study of the propeller as a means of lifting and built several experimental machines. In 1876, Enrico Forlanini fitted a gas-driven engine to a machine which rose to a height of 13m after a vertical take-off from the park in Milan. Louis Bréguet and Professor Richet built a helicopter in 1907 which rose to a height of about 2m above the ground, but it was very unstable. After World War I Demichen and Pescara in France, Juan de la Cierva in Spain, and Bothezat in the United States all built machines which were capable of staying airborne for about 10 minutes at a height of 5m. The Americans Sikorsky, Bell and Hiller made further contributions to the development of the helicopter, and since the 1940s it has achieved considerable importance in both civil and military life. The helicopter's speed is limited by the speed at which the propeller blades rotate, but it has the compensating advantage of being able to take off and land vertically, without runways or airports.

Did you know . . .

. . . that the first helicopter that really flew was a toy devised by Launoy and Bienvenu in 1784?

. . . that the usefulness of the helicopter was proved once and for all during the Vietnam War, when it was used for the transport and evacuation of troops?

The genius of Leonardo da Vinci was responsible for the design of the airscrew on the left, the ancestor of the helicopter. 'If it is rotated rapidly it will fly up into the air with a corkscrewing motion', said Leonardo.

On the right is the flying top built by the British inventor George Cayley (1843). Some years later the German Ganswindt invented a machine which was operated by a pedal.

An important success in the history of flight: the Spanish inventor Juan de la Cierva's first machine.

Juan de la Cierva's helicopter marked a vital stage in the machine's evolution. This is the first really practical helicopter, the Focke-Wolf (1937).

This helicopter was designed for practical use by the Russian-born Igor Sikorsky in the United States. It was tried out with great success during World War II for observation missions, antisubmarine surveillance, liaison purposes and rescue operations.

Like all other human inventions, the helicopter has continued to be improved right up to the present day. Many new methods of vertical take-off have been tried out. The illustration shows one such experimental model, Ryan's XC 142 (1964).

THE SUBMARINE

Since ancient times man has dreamed of being able to navigate under water. Aristotle, the Greek scholar of classical times, told stories of divers who could remain under water by wearing over their heads inverted vessels full of trapped air. A medieval document has been found showing a rudimentary diver's helmet. Attempts to invent a submarine were made during the eighteenth and nineteenth centuries, the first true submarine being invented by the American David Bushnell.

The German submarine proved an effective weapon during World War I, but it was not until World War II that the extent of its destructive powers was fully realized. The illustration above shows a submarine of the 1940s. In the picture below is the submarine built by the Spanish inventor Isaac Peral in 1886. It was 22m long and 2m wide. Like Monturiol, Peral had very little luck with his invention and received no official aid. At that time people could not see how the submarine could serve any practical purpose.

Sturmius' design for a diving-bell (1867). Other designs followed this one, but were equally unsuccessful.

Bushnell's submarine (1775), in the shape of a double tortoise-shell. It was used in the American War of Independence against the British.

Model of the *Ictineo*, the first submarine worthy of the name. It was built by Narciso Monturiol and made a successful dive in the waters of Barcelona harbour in 1859, staying submerged for 2½ hours. *Ictineo* means 'fish ship', and the vessel was indeed shaped like a fish and measured 7m from stem to stern. Without official support and faced by public indifference the inventor gave up in despair and sold his submarine for scrap.

The submarine has been and still is a terrible attacking weapon, the scourge of surface navigation, because of the terrifying power of its torpedoes which, once launched against an enemy ship, find their target with deadly accuracy. Left is shown one type of torpedo used during World War II. The German submarines, called U-boats, sank an enormous number of ships, taking such toll of the Allied Atlantic convoys that the supply of goods to Britain was in grave danger. By means of his periscope, the commander of a submarine could locate an enemy ship and launch his torpedoes accurately.

Man has long wanted to explore the ocean bed. The invention of the submarine has made it possible to build bathyscaphes capable of diving to great depths (up to 11,000m). Voyages made by Jacques Piccard and by many other scientists have added to man's knowledge of the deepest parts of the ocean. The picture shows the French submarine *Archimedes*.

The first naval use of atomic energy was to power a submarine. In 1955 the world's first atomic submarine, the *Nautilus*, was launched in the United States. Its fuel is a piece of uranium the size of a golf-ball, and it is capable of travelling at speeds of 20 knots for up to two years without refuelling. The picture shows the submarine breaking through the ice to surface at the North Pole. It is named after the *Nautilus*, the submarine in Jules Verne's novel *20,000 Leagues Under the Sea*.

X-RAYS

The discovery of X-rays, like so many other scientific achievements, was made more or less by chance. In 1895 Roentgen discovered the rays which are called after him and which he nicknamed 'X-rays' because he did not know what they were or where they came from. He became aware of their existence when he opened a drawer in his desk and found that some photographic plates had become fogged. He did not patent his invention, so it was freely available to anyone who could use it and soon became valuable in scientific, medical and technical fields. X-rays can penetrate to a considerable depth into substances which are opaque to ordinary light. The picture below shows one of the first X-ray machines.

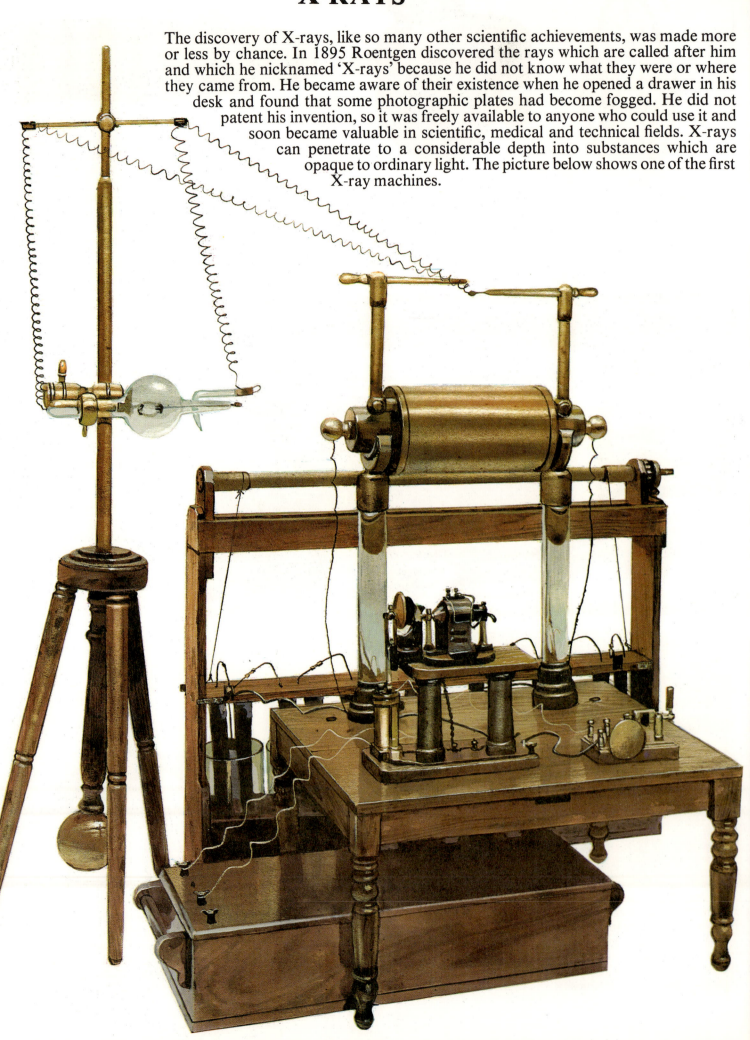

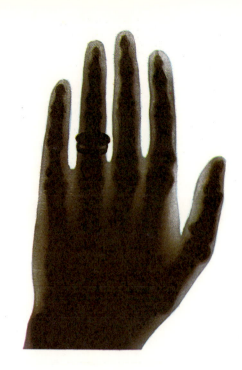

Roentgen discovered X-rays in 1895. The illustration on the right shows one of his first X-rays. While working on cathode rays he noticed that the tube was emitting mysterious radiations which could penetrate almost all solid substances and leave an impression on a photographic plate. This discovery has been tremendously important in the medical field and has also contributed to advances in every branch of physics.

Wilhelm, Conrad Roentgen (1845–1923), the German experimental physicist, who won the Nobel Prize for physics in 1901.

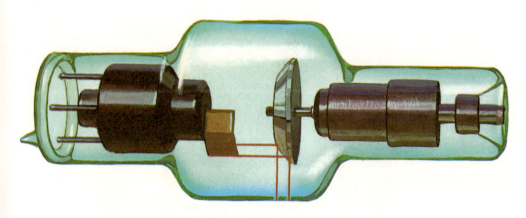

On the left is shown an X-ray tube. It consists of a sealed container inside which the pressure is reduced. This tube contains a cathode which emits a stream of electrons, a device to increase the speed at which they move and a metal target or anticathode which when bombarded by the stream of electrons becomes the source of X-rays.

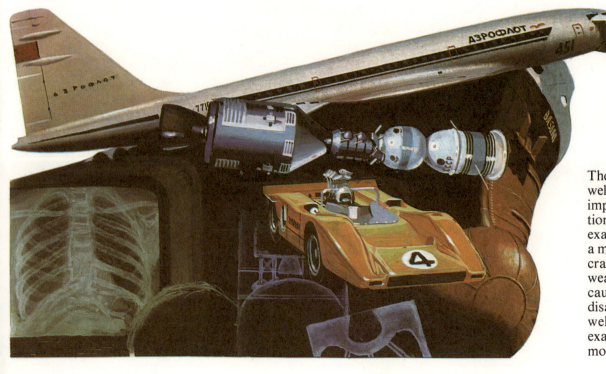

The medical uses of X-rays are well known, but they also have important industrial applications. They can be used to examine the key components of a machine, revealing any interior cracks or tiny holes which would weaken the part and perhaps cause it to break, resulting in a disaster. When materials are welded together, X-ray examination is often made of the most important joints.

THE MACHINE GUN

In 1865 the French officer Reffye invented a machine gun with a total of 25 fixed barrels which fired 125 to 150 missiles a minute. It was soon made obsolete by newer and quicker-firing models. In 1883 the American Maxim invented the automatic machine gun.

Although there were earlier versions, the modern machine gun and machine pistol were developed by Hotchkiss in 1914. His main aim was to make a gun which would give heavy fire over a limited area. The whole weapon was automatic and the cartridges were made up into belts which fitted one of the apertures of the machine gun. The gun was based on an American model invented by Gatling which could fire 100 missiles a minute. The idea of a rapid-firing weapon dates back to the days of the first firearms such as rifles and revolvers. Gatling's machine gun was used in 1865 during the American Civil War. There were other models by Montigny, Feldi, Nobel, Maxim, Gardner, Colt, Hotchkiss and Skoda. The machine gun has evolved through a variety of forms, but that used by the world's fighting forces today is a single-barrelled automatic weapon.

This machine, known as the multiple cannon (1450), is one of the earliest ancestors of the machine gun.

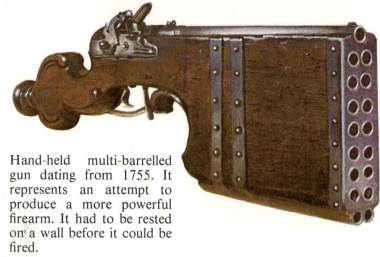

Hand-held multi-barrelled gun dating from 1755. It represents an attempt to produce a more powerful firearm. It had to be rested on a wall before it could be fired.

James Puckle patented this repeating weapon in 1718. It is closer to the machine gun than the two weapons shown above. One cylinder fired round bullets and another square ones, which were actually thought to be more effective against the enemy!

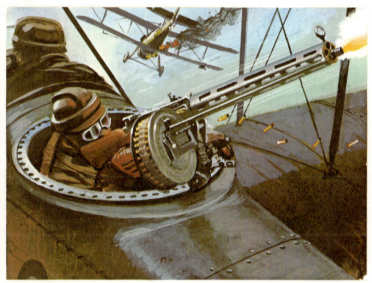

Once fighter planes were fitted with machine guns aerial warfare took on a new dimension. In early World War I aeroplanes the gunner had to fire across the propeller, which was therefore fitted with a deflector to prevent it from being damaged. Later the firing of the machine gun was synchronized with the propeller.

The development of the machine gun continued and military staffs tried to adopt the best model. Wartime experience proved that two or three men armed with an effective machine gun could halt a massive enemy attack. The picture shows a Maxim machine gun, adopted by the German army in 1908. The Maxim gun marked a new era in the evolution of the weapon. The gun is manned by two soldiers who are holding off an enemy attack.

American Bell P39 or Aircobra. This is a World War II fighter plane with a propeller, 6 Browning machine guns and a 20mm Hispano gun.

THE TANK

The tank is an armour-plated vehicle moving on caterpillar tracks and armed with a large gun. It was the answer to the tactical necessity of finding an offensive weapon capable of breaking through an enemy front. It can move over any type of ground surface. It made its first appearance on 15 September 1916 when the English used it on the battlefields of Flanders during World War I. In World War II the Germans formed divisions of armoured tanks with which they were able to make enormously successful lightning strikes in Poland, Belgium, France and Russia. There are many types of tank, including the Mark, the Panther, the Sherman, the T34, the Patton (shown below), the Centurion and the AMX.

Did you know . . .

. . . that the tank was first invented by the English, who kept its manufacture secret by having each component built in a different factory? The tanks were packed in cases and the rumour was put about that they were water tanks on their way to Africa. The English name has come into use in many languages.

. . . that the tank played such a decisive part in the German defeat in World War I that when the fighting was over the Germans said that they had been defeated not by Marshal Foch but by Marshal Tank?

The picture below shows a strange Roman war machine. Two little huts, each mounted on four wheels, were fastened together and pushed along by means of a tree trunk. It was a type of battering ram used against the enemy army, and in its day was an effective and devastating weapon.

The elephants used by Hannibal in his struggle against the Romans could perhaps be described as the ancestors of the modern tank. But the blind force of these beasts was difficult to direct and sometimes rebounded on the army using them.

Tanks were a decisive weapon in the two world wars of this century. Preceded by an artillery barrage, armoured tanks with their caterpillar tracks would move in and occupy enemy trenches.

War chariot invented by Leonardo da Vinci.

From 1914 onwards the tank played an important part in warfare. This picture below shows the powerful gun mounted on a revolving turret, the armour-plating and the caterpillar tracks.

Although the tank was originally developed as a weapon of war, as time passed and technical progress continued some of its features were applied to agriculture and to public works. Here is a tractor with caterpillar tracks.

PLASTICS

There can be no doubt that this is an age of plastics. The word covers a whole range of materials, used in the manufacture of a host of everyday articles from tools to garments. On this page there are a variety of familiar objects made of plastic. Synthetic materials are man-made substances which have never existed in the natural state. They come from the organic chemist's laboratory and include synthetic rubber, rayon, nylon, celluloid — and the whole range of plastics. Plastics are derived from hydrocarbon compounds often obtained from petroleum, and have found their way by now into every corner of modern technology and daily life. The development of synthetic materials began when Braconnet in France (1833) and Schoenbein in Switzerland (1845) prepared nitrocellulose. A whole series of new artificial substances then began to appear on the market, meeting every kind of human need.

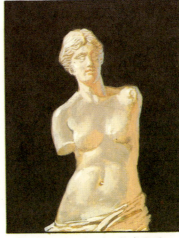

Ebonite is a type of plastic obtained by treating rubber with sulphur in the ratio 100:32. Its name is derived from the word 'ebony'. Many fountain pens are made of ebonite. It is also called vulcanite.

In 1869 an American, John Wesley Hyatt, discovered how to make celluloid from nitrocellulose and camphor. It was the first plastic to be commercially successful, being enormously useful to the photographic industry.

Casein plastic rivalled Bakelite but it softens in hot water. It was first manufactured in 1885 when pure casein was treated with formaldehyde. It was used as a substitute for horn, celluloid and ivory.

The Belgian chemist Baekeland discovered and patented the synthetic resin Bakelite in 1909. Unlike more modern plastics, it does not soften when heated. Electric plugs are made of Bakelite.

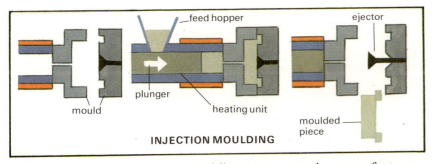

INJECTION MOULDING

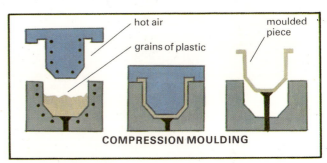

COMPRESSION MOULDING

Above is shown the injection moulding process used to manufacture thermoplastics such as the vinyls, polyethylene and plexiglass. Because they lose their rigidity when heated they are specially suitable for printed matter, laminating and the manufacture of threads. The process is shown starting with the empty mould and ending with the finished article.

The diagram above shows the commonest type of compression moulding used for thermosetting materials which, as their name indicates, reach the necessary degree of hardness when they are subjected to an irreversible heating process. Bakelite is one of these materials.

A type of injection moulding machine used for manufacturing plastic objects. Finely powdered plastic is put into the feed hopper at the top and heated so that it becomes soft and can be moulded. The cooling process is very quick and after a few seconds the mould is opened and the finished object removed.

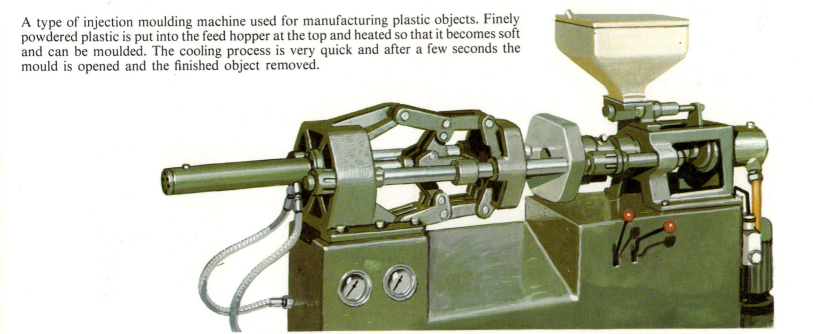

THE JET ENGINE

The jet engine works by ejecting a stream of gas at high velocity and high pressure, to produce a thrust. Not all inventions make their first appearance in their final form, but instead go through various stages of development. In the case of the jet engine these early stages can be traced right back to the inventions of the Frenchman Lenoir whose engine of 1863 was propelled by the expansion of air caused by burning gas, and Marcus who designed a petrol engine.

The German inventor Otto's internal combustion engine dates back to 1877. This engine was already famous when Daimler perfected it by reducing the weight without loss of power. He also devised an electronic ignition.

Did you know . . .

. . . that the motor industry benefited enormously when Daimler was sacked from his job, since he devoted himself entirely to the research which made him famous?

The original idea of the jet engine came from René Lovin (1908), but it was Henri Coanda who built the first model in 1909. A 40hp engine moved a turbine which replaced the propeller. It was a complete failure. However, it did manage to get off the ground, but Coanda took fright when he saw flames streaming from the engine, the plane lost height and crashed.

Serious work on the jet engine began in 1937. The Englishman Frank Whittle tried out a gas turbine, but it was the German Ernst Heinkel who made the engine a practical proposition with the first successful jet-powered flight in 1939. Experiments continued, and as is so often the case when new techniques are being pioneered, some were more successful than others.

DIFFERENT TYPES OF JET ENGINE

Pulse jet Simple, elementary and cheap. This was the first type of jet engine, used in the German V-1 missiles. It is not very efficient and today is rarely used.

Turbojet The commonest type of jet engine, and the first to use electricity. Heinkel's and Whittle's engines were of this type. The continuous combustion of the fuel causes the volume of gas to increase, moving the turbines which drive the compressors and develop the propulsive thrust.

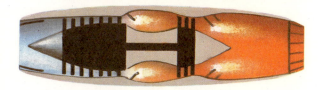

Turbojet with afterburner Resembles the previous type of engine, but combustion also takes place in a second chamber. Fuel is injected and burns using oxygen left over from the first combustion process. This gives a great increase of power, so this engine is used for high-speed aeroplanes.

Ram jet This type of engine has no moving parts. It will function only at high speed and therefore needs some form of assisted take-off. At high speeds it is a very efficient engine.

Turboprop (propeller turbine engine). Energy from the turbine is transmitted by means of reduction gears to the propeller, which cannot exceed 3,000 revolutions per minute. Used for civil aviation.

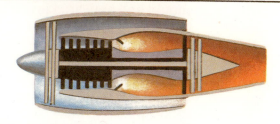

Turbofan Works in a similar way to other jet engines but with the addition of a fan or small propeller. Used by the great airlines of today because it is economical and low in noise.

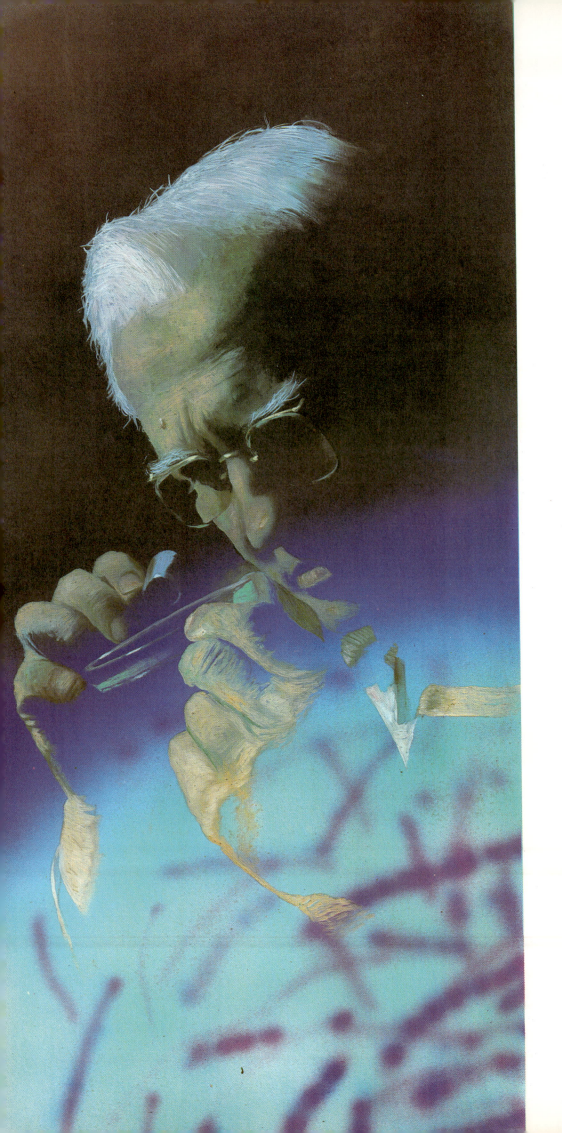

PENICILLIN

Most people have seen a crust of bread covered in green mould. This mould is actually composed of a mass of microscopic germs. Its scientific name is *Penicillium notatum.* These germs live on decaying organic matter. The most important name in the history of penicillin is that of the British doctor Alexander Fleming (1881–1955), although other men of medicine such as Florey and Chain made an outstanding contribution to the success of this antibiotic. Fleming was Professor of Bacteriology at St Mary's Hospital Medical School, University of London, where he had completed his own medical studies and decided to specialize in the problems of infection and healing of wounds. In 1922 he identified lysozyme, a bacterial ferment present in tears, saliva and white of egg, and six years later while working on this substance he accidentally discovered penicillin. He began a series of experiments on guinea-pigs, but his work aroused little public interest. Some years later his investigations were carried further by two researchers at Oxford, the Australian doctor Howard Florey and the chemist Ernst Chain, who isolated the green substance produced by the germs of mould and called it penicillin. In 1941 the two scientists gave the first injection of penicillin to a patient seriously ill with a blood infection. A powerful new medicine, destined to save many lives, had just been born.

Did you know . . .

. . . that while working in his laboratory Fleming noticed that a mould had appeared inside the lid of a dish containing cultures of bacteria, and that the bacteria were not reproducing in that spot?

. . . that Fleming realized at that moment that these germs could be used to cure diseases by preventing the development of the bacteria that cause them?

On the left: Penicillium culture. Notice its shape and colour. On the right: bacteria-free circles created by the penicillin mould in a culture of bacteria. The appearance of the culture is visibly altered when compared with the culture shown on the left.

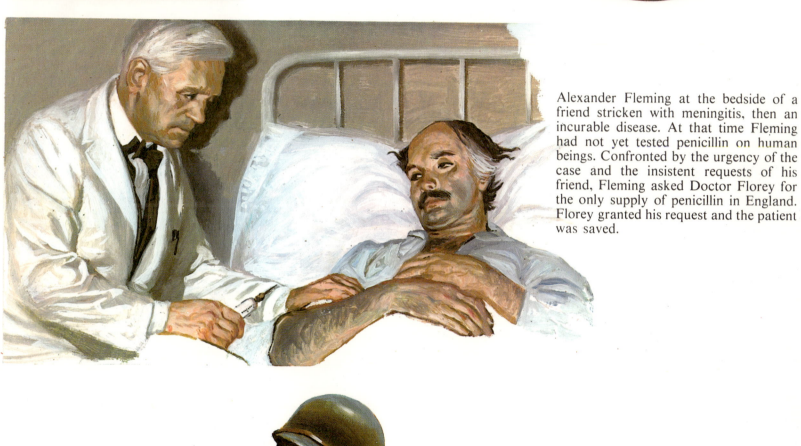

Alexander Fleming at the bedside of a friend stricken with meningitis, then an incurable disease. At that time Fleming had not yet tested penicillin on human beings. Confronted by the urgency of the case and the insistent requests of his friend, Fleming asked Doctor Florey for the only supply of penicillin in England. Florey granted his request and the patient was saved.

During World War II penicillin saved the lives of many servicemen. It was a kind of secret weapon.

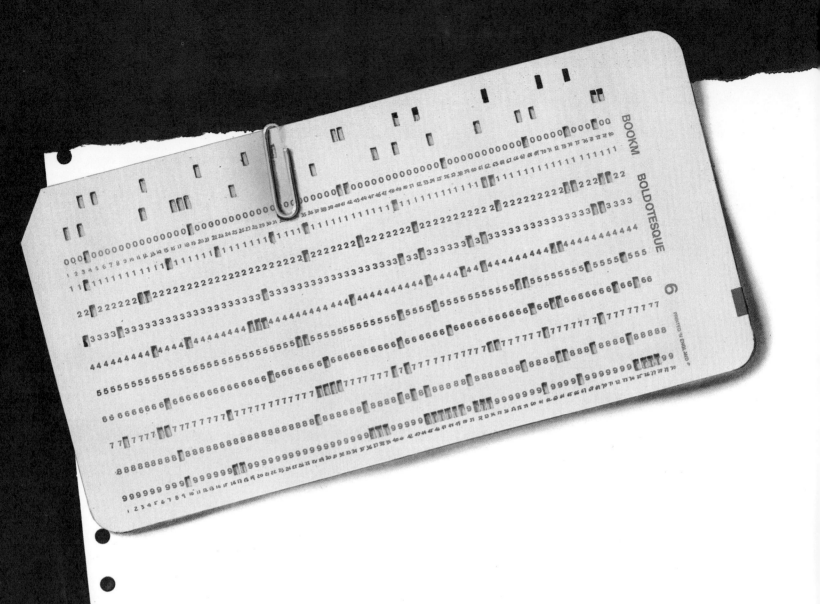

ELECTRONIC COMPUTERS

Electronic computers represent the most advanced achievement of modern science and technology, and bring us to the new science of cybernetics, the study of communication and control mechanisms in machines and in living creatures. The name comes from the Greek word *kybernetes*, a steersman, and this new-born science is largely the work of the American Norbert Wiener. The machines with which he worked were electronic computers. The system of punched cards (like the one shown above), which formed the basis of early computer development, dates from the early 1930s and revolutionized administration all over the world. Computers are used today in the most diverse fields: science, politics, economics and medicine, to name but a few.

The most elementary functions of a modern computer are memory, program, processor, input and output. Data and program are put into the machine by means of coded electrical impulses. The memory is composed of devices capable of storing the information in a form available to the processor. Various appliances are used including magnetic drums and magnetic tape. The input and output devices establish communication between the computer and the outside world. To be put into the computer the information may be recorded on punched cards or paper tape or magnetic tape. The corresponding input appliances will be card readers, paper tape readers or magnetic tape drives. The processor carries out the actions specified by the program.

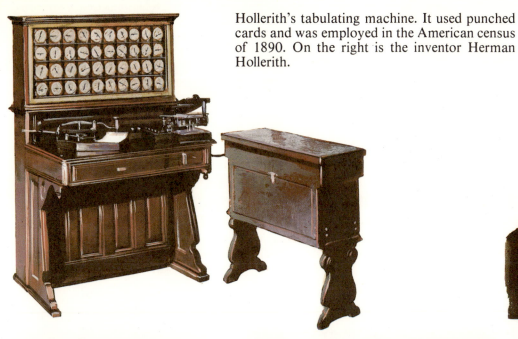

Hollerith's tabulating machine. It used punched cards and was employed in the American census of 1890. On the right is the inventor Herman Hollerith.

A modern card punch system. It is also possible for a computer to use a card punch system as an output device.

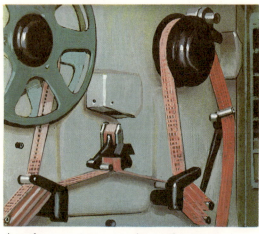

Another system consists of a continuous tape in which holes are punched to represent characters. It works like punched cards.

Magnetic tape systems. They are basically similar to paper tape systems but the characters are represented magnetically instead of by perforations.

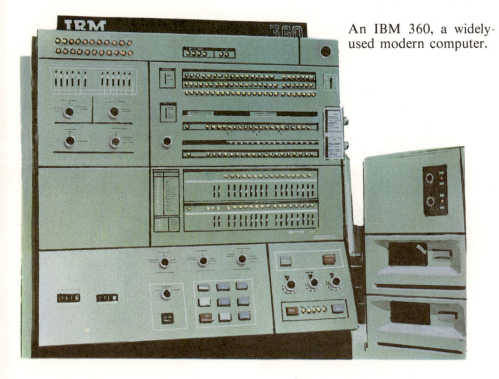

An IBM 360, a widely-used modern computer.

A modern computer terminal with a television screen. Answers to questions appear directly on the screen and there is no need for cards or paper tapes.